A Note to Parents

Eyewitness Readers is a compelling new program for beginning readers, designed in conjunction with leading literacy experts, including Dr. Linda Gambrell, President of the National Reading Conference and past board member of the International Reading Association.

Eyewitness has become the most trusted name in illustrated books, and this new series combines the highly visual *Eyewitness* approach with engaging, easy-to-read stories. Each *Eyewitness Reader* is guaranteed to capture a child's interest while developing his or her reading skills, general knowledge, and love of reading.

The four levels of *Eyewitness Readers* are aimed at different reading abilities, enabling you to choose the books that are exactly right for your children:

Level One – Beginning to read
Level Two – Beginning to read alone
Level Three – Reading alone
Level Four – Proficient readers

The "normal" age at which a child begins to read can be anywhere from three to eight years old, so these levels are intended only as a general guideline.

No matter which level you select, you can be sure that you are helping your child learn to read, then read to learn!

A DK PUBLISHING BOOK
www.dk.com

Project Editor Mary Atkinson
Art Editor Susan Calver
Senior Editor Linda Esposito
Deputy Managing Art Editor
Jane Horne
US Editor Regina Kahney
Production Kate Oliver
Picture Researcher Jo Carlill
Illustrator Norman Young

Reading Consultant
Linda B Gambrell Ph.D.

First American Edition, 1998
4 6 8 10 9 7 5 3
Published in the United States by
DK Publishing, Inc.
95 Madison Avenue, New York, New York 10016

Published in Great Britain by Dorling Kindersley Limited.

A catalog record for this book is
available from the Library of Congress.

ISBN 0-7894-4251-5

Color reproduction by Colourscan, Singapore
Printed and bound in Belgium by Proost

The publisher would like to thank the following for
their kind permission to reproduce their photographs:
Key: t=top, b=below, l=left, r=right, c=center
Bruce Coleman Collection: 13tr, 13cr, 32clb;
Holt Studios International: Primrose Peacock 14bl;
Telegraph Colour Library: Thompson Studio Recording 14tl;
Tony Stone Images: 10tl.

Additional photography by Peter Anderson, Jon Bouchier,
Jane Burton, Peter Chadwick, Gordon Clayton,
Philip Dowell, Mike Dunning, Andreas Von Einsiedel,
Dave King, Bill Ling, Kim Taylor, and Barrie Watts.

EYEWITNESS READERS

BEGINNING
1
TO READ

A Day at
Greenhill Farm

Written by Sue Nicholson

DK PUBLISHING, INC.

It is early in the morning.
The farm is quiet.

Then the rooster
begins to crow.

Cock-a-doodle-doo!

What a noise!

He wakes up
all the other
farm animals.

5

In the barn,
mother hen
starts to cluck.
One of her eggs
is ready
to hatch.

Cluck
Cluck

Peck, peck, peck!
A tiny chick breaks
through its shell.

More eggs crack open.
Five cheeping chicks
hatch out!

Cheep   Cheep   Cheep   Cheep   Cheep

Other farm babies
hatch from eggs too.

Mother duck has
six baby ducklings.

Quack
Quack

Mother goose
has four
baby goslings.

Honk
Honk

9

The ducks waddle
down to the pond.
They take
a morning dip.

Their wide,
webbed feet
push them
through the water.

The ducklings have soft, fluffy feathers called down.

down

Quack

Soon they will grow long, oily feathers to keep them warm and dry.

Geese like
to be near
water too.

Mother goose snaps up
grass and weeds
in her bright orange bill.

bill

Honk

She flaps her wings and honks
if anyone comes near
her goslings.

wing

The cows come
to the gate.
It is
milking time!

The farmer milks the cows.
He will sell the milk
for people to drink.

The cows go back
o the field
o munch grass.

Munch
unch

Munch
Munch

Other animals are hungry too.

A sheep
is nibbling hay.

So is a goat.

The pigs hunt
for food
in the barn.

One pig has her snout
in a bucket of corn!

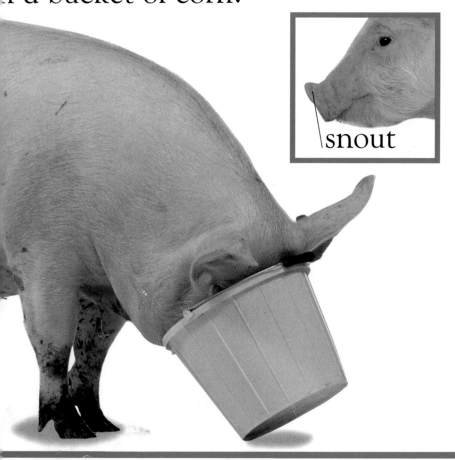

snout

The farm babies
tell their mothers
that they are hungry.

"Baa, baa!" cries the lamb
to mother sheep.

Baa
Baa

"Naa, naa!" cries the kid
to mother goat.

Naa

Naa

The piglets squeal and squeak.
Then they drink their mother's milk.

There are lots of babies
on the farm.

The cat has kittens.

Me

The kittens will grow up fast.

The mice
have babies too.

Squeak

Squeak

Meow

One day the kittens
will chase the mice!

Baby animals
love to play.

The kids butt each other
with their horns.

horns

The piglets like to roll in the mud.

Out in the fields,
the lambs skip and jump.
Skip, hop, jump!
One tiny hoof
follows another.

hoof

One calf has lost his mother.
"Moo! Moo!" he calls.
The mother cow calls back.
She is not
far away.

Moo
Moo

Mother horse
has a baby foal.
He is only
two months old.
But he can run fast

The foal races
around the field.
His mane blows
in the wind.

mane

All that running
makes the foal hungry.
He eats an apple.

Woof

In the afternoon,
the sheepdog
helps the farmer
round up the sheep.

Then the farmer
cuts the wool
off the sheep.

The sheep look
smaller and cleaner
without their wool.

Baa
Baa

wool

Evening comes. It is dark.
The farm is quiet.

The chicks ...

and the lambs ...

Zzzzzzz

and the piglets fall fast asleep.

The cat will keep watch
until the rooster crows again.

Farm Vocabulary

down
page 11

horns
page 22

bill
page 12

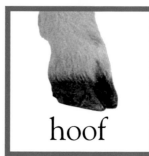
hoof
page 24

wing
page 13

mane
page 26

snout
page 17

wool
page 29

DK EYEWITNESS READERS

Level 1 *Beginning to Read*

A Day at Greenhill Farm
Truck Trouble
Tale of a Tadpole
Surprise Puppy!
Duckling Days
A Day at Seagull Beach
Whatever the Weather
Busy, Buzzy Bee

Level 2 *Beginning to Read Alone*

Dinosaur Dinners
Fire Fighter!
Bugs! Bugs! Bugs!
Slinky, Scaly Snakes!
Animal Hospital
The Little Ballerina
Munching, Crunching, Sniffing, and Snooping
The Secret Life of Trees

Level 3 *Reading Alone*

Spacebusters
Beastly Tales
Shark Attack!
Titanic
Invaders from Outer Space
Movie Magic
Plants Bite Back!
Time Traveler

Level 4 *Proficient Readers*

Days of the Knights
Volcanoes
Secrets of the Mummies
Pirates!
Horse Heroes
Trojan Horse
Micromonsters
Going for Gold!